The Dragon's Mountain

Book Two – The Hidden Village

Mark Mulle

PUBLISHED BY:

Mark Mulle

Copyright © 2014

Disclaimer

This is a work of fiction. Names, characters, businesses, places, events and incidents are either the products of the author's imagination or used in fictitious manner. Any resemblance to actual persons, living or dead, or actual events is purely coincidental.

Author's Note: This short story is for your reading pleasure. The characters in this "Minecraft Adventure Series" such as Steve, Endermen or Herobrine...etc are based on the Minecraft Game coming from Minecraft ®/TM & © 2009-2013 Mojang / Notch

Other books in The Dragon's Mountain Trilogy

Book Two – The Hidden Village

The three of us ran as fast as we could. There was not a doubt in our minds that Zeke and at least a few of his men were on our tail. We only hoped that they had lost a few minutes while ransacking the Greenfoot base.

We followed the direction in which the needle on the compass pointed, which actually took us right back to the Trent's base. It was a familiar path that we ran on and once again we did not stop for anything along the way. We ran and we ran, building no shelters and harvesting no resources, knocking monsters out of our way left and right, and stopping only for brief periods of time in order to eat and regain our strength.

Once we crossed the river and reached Trent's base, we saw the destruction that Zeke and his army had left behind. What was once a pretty cool desert base used to train and teach Minecraft noobs, was now a pile of rubble. The tall sandstone walls were now a block high and the houses and other buildings were holes in the ground, most likely destroyed by TNT explosions.

"Zeke is one poisonous potato," Jerry said.

"He sure is. That and some," Micah added.

"There were so many of them here. Fresh players, too. They just wanted to have fun time in Minecraft. They stood no chance against Zeke and his pack of griefers," I said.

"No point in sticking around too long. Spread out and see if you find anything useful. We will keep running for the next three days before stopping again," Micah said.

The three of us spread out and started looking around for useful stuff. I managed to find a few chickens and a pig. We burnt through a good portion of our food in our desperate run through the forest, so we needed every bit that we could get our hands on.

Micah only found some emeralds that were inside what had been a secret stash hidden bellow the floor of one of the houses. He also found a diamond sword and some bread loafs. Jerry found some wheat and a healing potion inside a chest. Apart from those, everything else was destroyed and looted. We couldn't find the brewing stand that they obviously used to brew the healing potion. Zeke's guys did a pretty good job in looting the whole camp.

After we regrouped, we pooled our resources together.

"The compass points that way," Micah said, pointing towards the east.

We knew that it was the east, because the sun was starting to rise.

I looked in that direction, trying to get a better idea of what would await us. The only thing that stood out was something that looked like a mountain, which had some rivers of lava flowing down from its peak.

"Maybe we could scout further ahead from up that mountain over there," I suggested.

"Not a bad idea, Mike. Let's roll," Micah said.

After that, we left the camp.

It turned out that the mountain was not only further than we first thought but it was also much bigger than we had expected it to be.

Once we reached the mountain we immediately started to climb up the rough terrain.

The mountain was mostly made out of sandstone with portions of sand from time to time. Cacti grew on its side and stuck out from time to time. Micah made sure to caution us not to touch any cactus, because they were quite dangerous and could cause us damage.

We climbed up the mountain, making sure to carefully cross the streams of lava that went down its sides.

When we were about halfway up to the top, we stopped climbing and started going around the mountain. When we reached the other side we stopped and scouted ahead.

The sun was slowly going down and I realized that our climb took almost all day.

The other bad news was that we could not see anything ahead apart from a vast sea of sand.

When the sun completely set, monsters started spawning. Zombies, creepers and skeletons began roaming at the foot of the mountain and on its sides.

"Is it me, or are there even more monsters than there were in the forest?" I asked.

"You are not far from the truth, Mike. From what I know, monsters spawn in greater numbers in the desert," Micah said.

"We better build ourselves a shelter," Jerry said.

"What about Zeke and his henchmen?" I asked.

"Jerry is right. We have to build a shelter. Zeke may be well armed and he may have a large group of fighters, but I don't think he'll risk moving through the desert at night, with all of those monsters creeping out there," Micah said.

"That is, if Zeke actually managed to keep up with us or if he has actually followed us," Jerry said.

"Trust me, there's a great chance that he did in fact follow us. Let's not underestimate him. Let's get indoors. We'll make plans later," Micah said.

Jerry took out his pickaxe and after we managed to find a good portion of the mountain that was made mostly out of sandstone he started digging a small two-block tunnel. The tunnel turned into a small room, a room just big enough for us to place our beds in. After the room was ready, we put some torches inside and then completely sealed the entrance with sandstone so that our small shelter would be camouflaged and hidden away from any eyes from outside. We placed our beds on the floor and went to sleep after we had our dinner.

When we woke up the next morning we stayed inside for a few more minutes in order to discuss our plans for the day and for the rest of our journey.

"So what now?" I asked.

"Where is your compass pointing?" Jerry asked Micah.

"Well, you won't like this, but it keeps pointing in that direction, straight into the desert. The trip will be a difficult one. We'll be out in the open," Micah said.

"We will have to ration our food. The desert is barren so we can't risk starving. Who knows how much we'll have to travel before we reach friendlier terrain," Jerry added.

"What about Zeke? Is he still following us?" I asked them.

"Well I have no idea…maybe he is," Micah said.

"Either way, we will see them if they do. The open desert doesn't leave them any place to hide," Jerry said.

"The open desert doesn't leave a place to hide for us, either," I added.

"We'll just have to risk it, then," Micah said.

"Right. So we run. We'll run for as long as we can, without stopping to build a shelter. If the monsters overrun us, we stop and take cover. But only if there is no choice," Jerry said.

"Ok. Let's head out," I said.

The three of us picked up our beds and torches and got out of there.

We spent the better part of the morning climbing down the side of the mountain and when we finally reached the base of the mountain we started running like madmen through the desert.

All that I could think about were our missing horses and how much easier this whole trip would have been if we were to have them now.

The whole walk through the desert was pretty depressing, if you ask me. There was nothing in sight for miles and miles, nothing to the left, nothing to the right and nothing in front. Behind us, the mountain was getting smaller and smaller as we advanced through the dune sea ahead.

From time to time we would encounter cacti. Other times, we had to either cross or to go around small lava pits or rivers.

Other than that the desert was pretty much empty.

The desert was empty of any mobs during the day.

The sun began to set but we showed no sign of stopping or even slowing down.

Once the sun had completely gone down, monsters began to spawn left and right.

At first, most of the monsters kept to themselves and didn't seem to notice our presence. But once we passed a creeper, it started hissing and within seconds it went up into a big explosion that drew the other monsters to us.

The monsters started immediately swarming to our location.

"Keep running! Keep running! Don't waste your time with the monsters!" Micah yelled.

I made sure to follow his instructions. But even more monsters were spawning up ahead of us. We zigzagged through the zombies, creepers and skeletons. Trying to dodge incoming fire from the skeletons and trying not to remain near any creeper in order to avoid getting blown to bits by it.

We managed to avoid the monsters and keep a healthy distance away from them but after a few minutes we reached a wide river of lava that prevented us from advancing. The river was pretty wide, probably more than a dozen blocks. The monsters advanced on our position. In the few seconds in which Micah, Jerry and I stopped to try and come up with a plan for escaping the situation we found ourselves in, the monsters got closer and closer, until the skeletons were close enough to shoot at us.

Incoming fire of arrows hit Jerry, almost knocking him into the lava.

"Guys! Run!" Jerry yelled.

"Where to?" I asked.

"Follow me! Let's run along the river! Stay close! Don't stop!" Micah yelled.

And so we did. We ran along the river with the monsters biting at our heels and under the rain of arrows that the skeleton archers kept launching in our direction.
Creepers kept closing in on us. We pushed them away with our swords and stuck to our route.

Micah led the way, I was right behind him and Jerry hanged back and made sure to protect our back.

Most of the monsters that were following us eventually stopped and gave up, but with every step that we took, more and more freshly spawned ones took their place.

Skeleton archers kept launching arrow after arrow and one of them managed to hit me. I got knocked back and Jerry caught up to me.

"Are you ok, Mike?" Jerry asked

"I'm fine, I almost fell into the lava,"   I answered.

"Let's keep moving," Jerry said.

And at that moment a creeper made its way to us from behind and exploded. The force of the blast threw Jerry and me forward.

When we came to our senses, we realized that our health bars were dangerously low. The good thing was that if the creeper was a bit more to the left, the force of the blast would have thrown us right into the lava.

Micah turned around and saw that Jerry and I were left behind. He took out his bow and arrow and started shooting at the nearby monsters, trying to provide cover fire for Jerry and I.

Micah was very good with the bow and arrow and he managed to provide us with enough cover fire so that we could eat a couple of pork chops and get our health bars back up.

After Jerry and I got our strength back up, we ran towards Micah and the three of us started running along the river of lava once again.

We ran and we ran, staving off the hostile mobs for as much as we could until we reached a portion of the river that was narrower than the rest of it. The river was now about six blocks wide.

Our desperate run was not only very dangerous, but it was also taking a toll on our resources, making us have to eat away our food supplies in order to keep our health bars up.

When we saw the river getting narrower we decided that we would build a bridge and cross over to the other side.

"Mike, you build the bridge while Micah and I cover you!" Jerry said.

At that moment, Micah equipped his bow again and started shooting arrows at the incoming monsters and Jerry stood nearby and used his sword to push back the monsters that managed to get too close.

I turned around and equipped a stack of cobblestone that I had in my inventory. By the way, this is the perfect way to illustrate just why it's a good thing to have a stack of cobblestone handy.

After I equipped my stack of cobblestone I started building the bridge. The first block that I tried to place didn't work, the lava was just too deep and it wasn't touching the bottom of the river. I then slowly and carefully walked towards the river and placed the cobblestone block right on the sand that was next to the river. I then started laying block after block and built myself a nice, one-block wide, cobblestone bridge that my friends and I could use.

I turned around and saw that my friends were completely surrounded by zombies, creepers and skeletons, almost to the point of being completely overrun by them.

"Come on! The bridge is ready!" I yelled.

From the other side of the river, Micah yelled back:

"Okay. We're coming! Keep the other side of the bridge clear so that we don't get trapped in the middle!"

He then turned to Jerry.

"Go! I'll keep them at bay and once I see you past the middle of the bridge, I'll make a run for it!"

"You go, Micah. I'll hold them off! Go!" said Jerry.

Micah shot down another zombie, then turned around and jumped onto the bridge.

"Suit yourself, but don't hand back too long, these guys are nasty," Micah told Jerry.

Micah started running towards me. Jerry slowly backed up to the first block of the bridge, constantly swinging his sword left and right, pushing back our attackers. The lava burned a fiery red in the night's darkness, like a sort of beacon that seemed to attract all of the monsters in the area.

I was standing on the other bank of the lava river, where there seemed to be less monsters, somehow, mostly zombies. I had my sword in my hand and I slashed away at the undead monsters. Some of them had armors on, or helmets; one even had a shovel in its hand.

When Micah finally crossed the river and jumped to my side to help me repel the monsters, Jerry finally decided to cross the river himself. He took another swing with his iron sword at an incoming creeper and then turned around and started running towards us. The creeper that Jerry had just hit started hissing violently and after less than a second, exploded with a large bang, destroying a part of the bridge. Luckily Jerry was already at a safe distance, halfway from reaching us.

Jerry finally managed to cross the bridge and jumped down next to us.

"Things look better on this side of the bridge!" Micah said, as he shot his last arrow at a zombie that was getting too close to us.

"Well, we can't linger here for too long, either," I said.

"Agreed," Jerry said, charging at the incoming zombies. "Come on! Follow me!"

But when Jerry took another swing at a small zombie that ran up to him, we heard a clacking noise and his sword completely fell apart, leaving him to hit the zombie with his bare hands.

Micah quickly equipped his own iron sword and jumped to Jerry's aid. I did the same and we started pushing the zombies back.

Micah then turned to Jerry and after briefly looking through his own inventory he dropped the gold sword that he had picked up from the chicken jockey that the two of us had killed in the forest. Jerry picked up the gold sword and the three of us started running and knocking monsters out of our way once more.

We managed to cover a good distance after regrouping. The night seemed to never end and after a small portion in which the road ahead seemed almost too clear, we ran into another cluster of monsters.

This time, we managed to go around them and prevent them from surrounding us. We knocked them back with our iron swords, wave after wave of zombies, creepers and skeleton archers.

Then, the sun started rising ahead and hope made its way into our minds, making us fight with even more might. But when we were thinking that the nightmare was just about over, we heard two loud clacking sounds, one after the other, and Micah's sword along with my own broke while hitting one of the zombies. The only one of us that still had a weapon was Jerry.

Micah and I both took out our axes and started using them to hack away at our attackers. But you see, axes aren't very effective as weapons in Minecraft as swords are. This not only means that they inflict less damage than swords but it also means that they degrade much faster than swords when used on anything but wood.

Our salvation came in the form of a giant yellow orb – the sun had finally risen and the light from it started burning the monsters around us.

We stopped trying to fight them and focused more on evading them. Within seconds, all of the monsters were completely destroyed, burnt away by the sun's rays.

The tree of us stopped running and regrouped.

"That was quite a night…" I said.

"You can say that again, Mike," Jerry agreed.

Our health bars were pretty low and we were starving. We went through our inventories and started eating whatever we had left from the night before. By the time we were finished eating, we realized that we had little to none provisions left.

I had a loaf of bread left, so did Micah, and Jerry still had a cooked pork chop.

"The situation looks pretty bad, guys," Micah said. "I don't know if these supplies will last us through this day, let alone this night."

"We'll find something…" I said.

"Well, it's good that you're so positive, Mike. But I really don't know how we're going to make it through…" Jerry said.

"Let's just keep going…okay? We've come this far and I personally don't see any other option," I told them.

There was a brief moment of silence.

"Mike's right. We have come this far, we can't give up now. Let's press on," Micah said.

Jerry nodded.

And so the three of us started walking through the desert, under the scorching sun. We refrained from running, though. Running makes you hungry much faster than walking does and we didn't exactly have enough food to afford getting hungry.

We walked silently through most of the day, getting hungrier and hungrier along the way.

"I really can't believe that this is happening. Truly," Micah said.

The sun was slowly going down.

"I mean…here we are, in the desert. Starving," Micah continued.

"Shut up, Micah!" Jerry said.

"No, really. We are out here, walking through the desert, starving like a bunch of newbie nooblers. No offense, Mike!" Micah said.

"What? What is that supposed to mean?" I asked Micah.

"Well, you know. I mean…we've faced Herobrine! We foiled his plans, defeated his army of darkness, and sent him back to wherever he came from. Does that count for nothing? I was a leader of a serious clan! I led my men with great wisdom!"

"Shut up, already!" Jerry yelled.

"I had a whole village to myself! A beautiful camp! And right now I'm about to starve to death with two noobs…You know even if we respawn back at that mountain, we will starve to death again and again and again and again…"

"Oh my gosh! Shut UP!" yelled Jerry, once again, but louder.

"This journey is pointless and it's going to be the death of me. You two…"

But distant growling suddenly interrupted Micah's little speech. The growling became more and more intense. And in a few seconds we found ourselves running away from what looked like a giant horde of zombies and creepers and skeletons.

While we were busy being annoyed by Micah's complaints, the sun had set completely and monsters had started spawning all around us. We now found ourselves running desperately, while at the same time getting hungrier and hungrier.

We kept running for as much as we could, until we finally stopped.

"There's no point in running anymore, guys," said Micah.

"That's true. But if I'm going out, I want to go out fighting," I said.

"Truer words have never been spoken!" Jerry said.

"So I guess that's it, boys. It was a nice little trip we took. Too bad we didn't manage to reach the treasure."

And at that moment we saw a dark figure move in the shadows, next to the pack of hostile mobs that was about to obliterate us. The dark figure that was the size of a player started throwing potions at the monsters, taking them down quickly, one after the other. He then started setting them on fire, while running towards us.

By the time the dark figure reached us, we saw that he was a player, just like us. He had a full set of enchanted diamond armor, enchanted diamond breastplate, diamond helmet, grieves and boots. When he got next to us, he unequipped his flint and steel that he used to set fire to and around the monsters and switched it with an enchanted diamond sword. He swung left and right and the monsters died almost instantly.

After he cleared all of the incoming monsters he turned around and looked at us.

"Howdy! What are you three doing so far into the desert?"

"We were traveling..." I told him.

"Travelling? In the desert? In the middle of the night?" the player asked laughing.

"We are very, very hungry. We ran out of provisions…we're starving," Micah told him.

The player opened his inventory and took out three pork chops and threw them on the ground.

"Here you go, guys. You can thank me later," the player said.

The three of us picked up the pork chops, one pork chop each, and ate them in a flash.

"Thanks, man! Really! You're a swell guy!" Jerry said.

"Yeah, well, that I am. I don't get a lot of people traveling around these parts. That's why I like it. I'm Ken, by the way," said the player.

"I'm Jerry. This is Micah and that's Mike. It's a pleasure to meet you, Ken," Jerry said.

"I'm sure that it is, Jerry. Pork chops are great for making friends, ha!" Ken laughed. "I assume that you guys don't have a place to crash, now do you?" Ken asked.

"No, actually we don't," Micah said.

"Well, come with me," Ken said.

"Wait…I have to tell you: we may be followed by a hostile clan. They pillage and plunder and kill anyone who they come across," I told Ken.

"Hmm…well, it's good that you decided to tell me. Then don't come with me…Nah, I'm just joking, you can crash at my place until you get your strengths up. Hostile clans don't really scare me. I can handle my own. Come on, before more monsters show up. The night is still young and these places have a tendency to spawn unusually large amounts of monsters at night. Personally, that's why I like them so much. Hehe!" Ken said.

We followed Ken for a few minutes until we reached a huge mountain. We walked up to the side of the mountain, right behind Ken. The mountain wall was very abrupt, and we could see no visible path that we could have used to climb up.

Ken walked right up to the mountain wall and took out a diamond pickaxe and destroyed a sandstone block. Behind the block was a weird looking gray block. Ken seemed to mess with the strange block, putting something – only he knew what – inside the block. A moment later, the sandstone blocks within the walls started shifting around in a pattern to reveal a tunnel.

"Well, don't just stand there, gents! Come on in!" Ken said.

So we stepped inside the tunnel. Behind us, Ken activated the gray block again and the tunnel sealed itself back up.

"Wait here a second," Ken said.

He disappeared for a brief moment and then returned to us.

"I had to hide the dropper. You know, that thing in the wall…anyway. Follow me," said Ken, while walking down the tunnel.

We walked through that tunnel for a couple of minutes and at the end of it we reached a village. Yup, a village…

I looked around at the strange view that was in front of me. The whole village was right inside the mountain. I'm not talking about a player-made village. No, this was a proper village, with villagers and everything. The big-nosed villagers were inside the houses, looking at us from behind their doors and windows as we walked by.

I looked up and saw the night sky.

"This is amazing!" I said out loud.

"It is, isn't it?" Ken asked.

"How did…Wow…How did all of this…"

"Well, I've been playing Minecraft for a long time. In fact, when I first spawned, the world was really, really empty. I mean, there were a lot fewer types of blocks and mobs and items and everything. I found this village out here in the desert right next to a mountain and, well, I sort of built the rest of the mountain around it," Ken said.

"This is just plain crazy," Micah said.

"Micah!" said Jerry.

Ken laughed.

"No, he's right. It is crazy. But I enjoyed doing it. I'm a patient guy and I like to build stuff. A couple of buddies helped me build the whole thing, though. It still took a whole lot of time and even more effort, but I find that it's worth it. We kept it secret from other players. It was our little secret, our secret base."

"Yeah…little…" said Micah.

Ken laughed again and went on with his story.

"My friends stopped playing Minecraft a long time ago and I've been here by myself since then. I've been to the Nether a whole lot of times. I've even managed to slay the Ender Dragon, by myself. It was all good fun. I love Minecraft."

"You're not a fan, Ken. You're a fanatic," Micah said, laughing.

"I suppose I am. Check this out!" Ken pointed at the tall black tower in front of us.

And as we looked ahead we saw a tall black tower, looking down on the village.

"Pretty insane isn't it?" Ken asked.

"What is that thing?" I asked.

Micah ran up to the tower and looked straight up.

"Is that thing made out of…"

"Obsidian. Yup!" Ken said.

"That must have taken you…"

"A whole lot of time, Micah. But it looks cool, doesn't it?" Ken asked.

The tower was black, with purple shades to it and a large fire burning at the top of it. The door to the tower opened up in a similar way to the door to the whole base.

"Come in. I'll show you to your chambers," Ken said.

Once we stepped inside, we saw that although the tower looked dark and menacing from outside, the inside was pretty welcoming. The floors were made out of dark wood and the walls were also lined with wood, but of a much lighter color. There were different paintings hanged on the walls and blue and red carpets covered the floor. Bookshelves covered the walls from time to time and there were armor stands with chainmail, leather, gold, iron and diamond armor on display. Chests were everywhere you looked and so were potted plants and cacti. The guy even had jukeboxes in every room.

"Welcome, guys, to my humble abode. What do you think?" Ken asked.

"It's beyond awesome!" I said.

Jerry and Micah were still looking around the place, marveling at the amount of cool items that Ken had on display.

"Come on up to my study. It's my favorite room, you know. I spend most of my time there, when I'm not wandering through the desert, that is," Ken said.

We walked up five or six stories; the stairs seemed to never end. When we reached what seemed to be the top level of the tower we walked inside a huge room.

The room's floor was made out of nether bricks, and the walls were made out of stone bricks. There were torches all around the room and a big chandelier that was made out of a dark red fence hanged from the tall ceiling, although the rest of the rooms in the tower were lit using glowstone and glowstone lamps. On one of the walls of the room there was a nether portal. Inside the room there were countless bookshelves, anvils, brewing stands and enchanting tables, along with a jukebox and several iron cauldrons filled with water and dozens upon dozens of furnaces in which the fire was burning.

The whole room, and actually, the whole tower had me thinking of all the fantasy stories about wizards that I had ever read.

Ken stopped in front of a large window that looked down at the village.

"So, guys. How do you like my village?" Ken asked.

"It's awesome," I said.

"Don't mind Mike, he's just an impressionable noob," Micah laughed.

"But it is awesome," Jerry added.

"Thanks. Hearing that makes my work a bit more worthwhile. So, guys…what were you doing out in the desert?"

"We were traveling," Micah said.

"Can I ask where to?"

"Uh…you know. We were exploring…" Micah hesitantly answered.

"Exploring? Out in the desert? Of all places?"

"Yeah."

"Hmm…you were honest before when you said that you might have been followed and that you might be in danger. So, I don't really buy the exploring story," Ken said.

I kind of felt bad about lying to him. I mean, the guy took us in, no questions asked. He took us into his secret village, of all places. I mean sure, he was confident that we would pose no danger to him, but still.

"We're on an adventure, a quest," I said.

I immediately expected to be yelled at by Micah. Luckily he didn't yell at all.

"Oh! A quest? That sounds exciting. What is the quest for?" Ken asked rather anxiously.

"Uhm…we're looking for a treasure; one that is inside a mountain," I said.

"Really? I think I know what you're talking about," Ken said.

Micah started fidgeting in his inventory and walking around the room, slowly backing away from Ken and the rest of us.

"Oh, it's a childish quest. The treasure isn't that big anyway. I mean, we ourselves aren't that sure that it exists or anything. I mean…"

"Oh come on, Micah. I have no interest in stealing the treasure for myself, in case that's what you're thinking," Ken said.

"You don't?" Micah asked.

"Nope. I have no use for it. Do I look like I even need the treasure?" Ken asked.

"Well…don't you want to go out on an adventure?" I asked him. "You're free to join us. You look more than well suited to go on such an adventure."

Ken laughed out loud.

"I do. And I am probably one of the most well suited players to go after that treasure. But I'm not that interested in doing so."

"Why not?" asked Jerry.

"Well, I'm working on stuff right here. What you see above ground is not even half of what lies underground. I have my experiments and machines to work on. I used to travel a whole lot, you see. That's how I got to have all of which you see in this village. I thought about getting that treasure for myself a while ago. But meh, I don't know," Ken said.

"So you won't join us, then?" I asked Ken.

"I'm afraid that I won't, no. But I know a great deal about it, though," Ken said.

"We would very much appreciate it if you would share some of that information with us," said Jerry.

"Do you have a golden compass?" Ken asked.

A brief moment of silence came up, before Micah answered.

"Yeah, I have one right here."

"Cool. I have a couple of them myself, but it's good that you have one. So, let's see…Hmm…The treasure is pretty far from here, I'm afraid. You'll have to walk another two days through the desert. Then, you'll reach the sea. Yep! The sea. And I'm afraid that you'll have to cross that sea, too. You'll need boats for that and plenty of food, too. Be careful not to hit anything while sailing, though. The sea is really deep and if you lose your boat and don't have a spare…well…Anyway, then, you'll reach the tundra. It's freezing there so expect a lot of snow, wolves and that stuff. I don't really know how much you have to walk from there. Once you reach the mountain you will find a village. What's inside the village, again, I have no idea. Personally, I would say that you expect the worse. Then there's the mountain. If you think that this mountain is big, think again – that one is huge. It will literally take you four days to reach the top of it. I don't know who built that giant thing, because it's not generated. I think that some old admin may have built it with codes and stuff, who knows? Some said it's a glitch, some say Herobrine, some say Notch, others…. well, you get the point. The idea is that the mountain takes four days to climb and that there are dangerous things lurking up there. You'll need some strong items to make it safely. What you'll find up there, I don't know. But I'm guessing that there you will find the treasure. Finally, the last thing I know, well, at least I heard this rumor, is that there is an Ender Dragon somewhere on that mountain – a white one. And that's basically it."

Jerry, Micah and I stood there silently. After Ken finished his story we looked back and forth at each other for a second and then back at Ken.

"How do you know all of this?" I asked.

"I've been around here far more than anyone else, guys. You hear things, you see things, and sometimes people tell you things. You've got to sort out fact from fiction for yourself, but you get the idea. I've been to that place before. I mean I've crossed the sea, but I had no interest in the mountain. I was pursuing other things. There used to be a lighthouse somewhere along the shore. I didn't use a golden compass then, though. Anyway, if you stumble into a lighthouse along the way and if there are players still living there, make sure to tell them you know me. That way maybe they will help you," said Ken.

"Wow...it turns out that we have quite an impressive adventure ahead of us, guys," Micah said.

"Yeah and so far we've managed to almost starve to death in this desert," Jerry added.

"Hey, don't beat yourselves up, guys. Come on, I'll walk you to your chambers and you can have a good night's sleep. I'll have some food ready for you in the morning and we'll talk then," Ken said.

"Well, thank you again Ken," I told him.

"Meh, don't mention it, I was quite bored. Company is nice once in a while," Ken confessed. "Who is following you, by the way?"

"Oh, some knucklehead with an angry clan at his command. They want to reach the treasure too, and destroy the three of us along the way," Micah answered.

"Hmm...you're safe here. Those guys sound like real jerks," said Ken.

"Are you sure that you can't help us deal with them?" I asked.

"I'm sorry but I don't really get involved in clan stuff or in player's affairs really. I know it sounds weird, but I enjoy staying away from that stuff. I'll help you guys as best as I can. But we will talk about this tomorrow morning," Ken said.

After our conversation, Ken walked us to our room, where he already had beds laid out. Each of us got into our beds and for the first time in a whole lot of days, we felt safe.

The next morning Ken came by our room and dropped off cooked veal, mutton and pork chops and some bread. The meal was fit for a king. We all ate up and then Ken walked us through the village. The village looked like any normal village, the villagers planted their crops and harvested them, and they walked around town and got into their houses from time to time. The houses looked perfect – with none of the flaws that you would expect from a normal generated village. The enclosures were filled to the brim with animals. After the tour, Ken insisted that we stay another night and we did.

Later that evening, Ken informed us that he had taken a look around the mountain and that he could not see any trace of players or Zeke and his evil lot.

The next morning we had to leave, Ken would have welcomed us to stay for as much as we'd like, but the three of us decided that we could not waste any more time.

When we woke up, Ken took us through a different tunnel that took us on the other side of the mountain. He said that from that point we would have clear path to the sea.

Before letting us head out Ken stopped us for a few minutes.

"Well, it's been a pleasure to meet you guys. I thought about it and I decided to help you guys out a bit on your journey. But only on one condition, and I mean it!" said Ken.

"What's the condition?" I asked.

"I'll help you on the condition that when you finish your adventure, you guys come back and visit me and tell me all about it. I want tons and tons of details. Got it?" asked Ken.

"For sure, Ken. That's the least we can do!" I said.

"Oh, and bring me back some diamonds and emeralds, too. That always helps," said Ken.

"We'll be sure to bring you a good amount of diamonds, Ken," Micah said.

"And emeralds," Jerry added.

"Cool. Now listen here, guys. I've prepared a mule for you. It has containers on it and they are full of food, enough to last you until you reach the mountain and back. I've also packed you some iron swords, torches and two bows and a stack or two of arrows," Ken said.

"Wow…that's really a whole lot of things, Ken! It's too much!" I told him.

"Yeah, well, trust me, you'll need it! Oh and I've also given each one of you a full set of diamond armor and enchanted diamond swords," said Ken.

I couldn't believe what I was hearing.

"And some useful potions. Nothing major. Just something to help you along the way. Make sure that you clear your inventory before you reach the sea, so that you can store everything. Empty the containers on the donkey and leave it tied up, I'll find it. And that's about it. Safe journey, guys! I hope I'll see you soon!" said Ken.

We thanked him a dozen times for his help and after that, we went on our way.

That whole day we couldn't stop talking about all the cool things that we saw in Ken's village and about how cool he was in giving us all the stuff that he did. Neither of us had ever met someone like Ken before. He truly was a wizard – I know how geeky that sounds, you don't have to tell me.

The first day through the desert wasn't that eventful. When the night came, we settled down and built ourselves a shelter and even kept the donkey indoors with us. At that point we knew that we were pretty safe from any attack from Zeke and his goons.

The second day we kept walking in the same direction, following the needle on the golden compass. Again, the day went on without any major events. When the sun set, we had reached our destination and we built our camp on the seashore.

That night we rationed our foods and emptied the containers that the donkey carried. We rationed our food and we divided up our supplies. We built a crafting table and crafted ourselves three boats and three spare ones, in case something were to happen to the first ones. When the morning came, we took down our camp and left the donkey tied up on the shore, just as Ken told us to do.

We then placed our boats in the water and sailed off. The water got deeper and deeper but, nonetheless, it remained peaceful. Our three boats sailed smoothly over the deep blue water. Behind us, the land got further and further and beneath us, the black and grey octopuses swam in every direction.

The day went by without any events. We sailed side by side, in the direction in which the needle on the golden compass pointed. We spent most of our time talking about various things; most of the discussion was about our previous adventure and about Herobrine. When the sun had completely set we started talking about the adventure that we were on and about what we were going to do with all the treasure that we would find.

"Should we stay there? I mean after we find the treasure?" Micah asked.

"I don't know. Do you mean should we stay near the mountain or…" Jerry asked.

"Yeah. Should we stay there, near the mountain after we get the treasure? I mean, build a base and stuff," Micah asked again.

"I don't know. What would we even do with all of that loot?" I asked.

"That's the least of our concerns, Mike," Micah said.

"Well, I propose that we get all of that treasure, first, and then we can think about what we should do next. I mean we don't really have a lot of uses for all the diamonds, emeralds, gold and whatnot. " I proposed.

"We could build ourselves a town, something much bigger than just a village or a camp. We could create our own clan and use all of that loot to trade and build a lot of cool stuff," Jerry said.

"We could even build a railroad system. I've always wanted to build something like that," I said.

"We could do that, but..." Micah started saying.

"What's that?" I asked, pointing to something in the distance.

Micah and Jerry turned their boats around and looked at what I was pointing.

As we got closer, the small shape in the distance started growing and in a matter of seconds, the shape started turning into a small island. The island must have been somewhere along the lines of twenty by twenty blocks and made out of dirt for the most part. A small stone house was built in one of the corners of the island and most of the island was covered with wheat crops.

When we got closer to the island we could see that the small mass of land that was above the water was basically just the tip of a huge mountain that was submerged under water. The island was well lid by torches placed all around the wheat crops and around the house.

Once we got a few blocks away from the island, a player came out of the house, waving his hands in the air and yelling at us.

"Hey! You there! You three!" the player yelled.

The three of us stopped in our tracks and looked at each other.

"What do you think, guys?" I asked Jerry and Micah.

"I don't know...we're in kind of a hurry," Micah said.

"Maybe he's stranded here. We should go and talk to him. We're pretty well equipped ourselves. I don't think that he's a threat. I doubt that it's an ambush," Jerry said.

"I agree with Jerry. We should check the island out and talk to this guy," I said.

"There you have it: two votes against one, Micah. The group has decided," Jerry said.

"Oh, so we're voting, now, are we? Fine! Let's talk to the stranded guy. But if it's a trap or something, just remember that I cautioned against it. Don't get mad at me when I'll be saying that I've told you so," Micah said.

We then sailed further towards the island.

Once we got closer to land, we got out of our boats carefully so we wouldn't smash them against the shore and stepped on dry land for the first time that day.

The guy that was on the island came up to us to greet us.

"Hey, guys! How are you doing?" he asked.

"Hi. We're just passing by. What are you doing on this island in the middle of the sea?" Micah asked the guy.

"Well, I spawned here. My name's Tom_Cat7," said the guy.

"Cool. We'll call you Tom, then," Micah said.

"What's your name?" Tom asked.

"I'm Micah, that's Jerry and that's Mike," Micah answered.

"Nice to meet you. I heard that this world was full of players. Imagine my luck to get spawned smack dab in the middle of the sea," Tom said.

"Why didn't you leave the world?" Jerry asked.

"Well, I'm not the kind of Minecraft player that gives up on a challenge, man. I've been living on this island for a full week I think. It wasn't easy but I made it work," Tom proudly said.

"How?" I asked.

"Oh, Mike, you noob…" Micah said.

Tom laughed.

"It isn't easy. When I spawned on the island there was some grass growing around the place. The biggest threat was starving to death, so I knew that I had to find a food source. I cut down all of the grass, grabbed the seeds and made myself a small wheat farm, maybe five blocks worth of wheat at first. When I spawned I had a bonus chest. Luckily it had some blocks of wood in it, enough to build myself a crafting table and some tools. In hindsight, I should have built myself a boat, but I figured that I could starve to death if the mainland would have been too far. Anyway, I managed to mine quite a bit. That wasn't easy at all. I kept switching mining with my pickaxe with mining with my bare hands, in order to keep my pick from getting worn down. I actually managed to find a small abandoned mineshaft yesterday. I explored most of it. I found a lot of useful things so I guess my perseverance paid off," Tom recounted.

"Wow. That's really cool," I said.

"Yep. It is. It really goes to show that if you don't back down from challenges in Minecraft. I found a lot of stuff down the abandoned mineshaft: carrots, lots of wood, bread, coal, iron; a lot of good useful stuff," Tom said.

"So I guess you're not interested in going to the mainland," Jerry said.

"Why did you signal us, then? You don't seem to be in any danger," Micah said.

"Yeah, well, I really came to this world in order to play Minecraft alongside other players and so far, I haven't really see anyone. I got excited," Tom confessed.

"What if we were looters or griefers?" I asked.

"Yeah, I didn't really think that through. Are you looters or griefers?" Tom asked.

"No, in fact we are not looters nor griefers. We are adventurers," I answered.

"Nice. Can I come along with you guys on your adventures?" Tom asked.

"You can come with us to the mainland. You can decide if you still want to tag along with us on our current adventure once we reach the mainland," Micah said.

"That sounds great. I'll be ready in ten minutes. Let me gather my stuff," Tom said.

"Ok, sure. Just make it snappy. We are in kind of a hurry," Micah said.

"Sure. Ten minutes. Wait here," Tom said.

After that, he turned around and ran inside his small stone house. We couldn't see where the entrance to Tom's mine was but we assumed that it was somewhere inside his house.

Ten minutes or so later, Tom came out running from inside of his house, wearing a full set of iron made out of iron and carrying an iron armor in his hand.

"I'm ready," Tom said while walking up to us.

"Great. Do you have a boat, Tom?" I asked.

"Yeah. I crafted myself one a minute ago," Tom said.

"Let's go then!" Micah said.

The sun was already rising.

Micah was the first one that jumped into the boat and sail away. We hurried to our boats, jumped in and followed Micah.

Micah managed to place a bit of distance between him and Jerry, Tom and I. I suspected that he did that in order to equip his golden compass without Tom seeing it. Micah clearly didn't trust Tom yet.

We sailed for the rest of the day and the next night, stopping to eat from time to time.

When the sun rose again, we saw land clear up ahead. Not only did we see land ahead, but we also could see a rather tall tower on the shore – the lighthouse that Ken was talking about.

As we got closer we could see the lighthouse better – it was built out of stone bricks and dark wood and it must have been at least thirty blocks tall. At the top of the lighthouse there was a large cup made out of stone bricks in which a giant fire kept burning, lighting up the sky.

"Let's head over to the lighthouse and check that out, guys. Be careful and keep your swords close. Ken said that he knew those guys but nonetheless we should be careful," Micah said.

So we strode across the water in our small wooden boats and set out on dry land somewhere near to where the lighthouse was.

As we looked further ahead deep into the coast of the mainland we saw that the earth gradually got more and more covered with thick layers of snow. The coastline though wasn't, patches of sand and grass ran along the shore.

We walked up to the lighthouse and saw that it had four small houses next to it. The houses were made out of bricks – normal, regular bricks that you make out of clay - and had dark colored wood roofs. The sky was cloudy and the light that fell over the land gave the scenery a weird, somewhat scary feeling to it.

The houses seemed empty, although there were torches all around them. The small buildings were joined together with a stone fence. On the inside of this small courtyard we saw a couple of dogs that were tied to wooden fence posts. There was a small pumpkin patch on the side of the encampment and some wheat crops that were ready for the picking, next to a small pond. The place looked eerily abandoned.

Once we got closer to the lighthouse and to the small houses, the dogs started barking aloud. The silence that was heavily weighing on the whole scene got suddenly disturbed when the loud barks echoed through the air.

Out of the blue, the iron door to the lighthouse opened and a player wearing a white leather armor and blue leather boots came out with an iron sword in his hand.

"Oi! What are you lot doing here? Have you come to pillage my lighthouse?" the player asked.

"We don't want to pillage your lighthouse. We are just passing by," Jerry answered.

"I'll let my dogs loose on you if you're lying, I will. Don't think that I won't," the player cautioned.

"Well, keep your dogs leashed, man. He told you already, we're just passing by! We don't want any trouble. We, uh, we know Ken. He told us to tell you that we are friends of his," Micah said.

"Friends of Ken, you are, eh? What does he call his little village, then?" the player asked.

Micah, Jerry and I turned to each other. None of us had any idea how Ken called his village.

Micah turned around and decided to give him an answer.

"He didn't tell us. He didn't call his village anything while we were there," Micah told the guy.

"Hmm…didn't call his village anything, eh? Well, you're right, you are. He doesn't have a name for his village, that weird old hermit. Come on upstairs then. Are you hungry?"

The three of us sighed with relief, while our friend Tom had no idea what we had been talking about.

The four of us then followed the guy upstairs to his lighthouse. We climbed what seemed to be an infinite numbers of stairs that spiraled up to the top of the lighthouse where the guy lived.

Once we reached the living quarters, the place wasn't that bad after all.

"I'm Ben, by the way. I'm the resident of this here lighthouse. How do you know Ken, eh? And most importantly why are you here?" asked Ben.

"Well, we were out in the desert, starving and Ken took us in. He gave us some supplies and helped us on our way," Jerry said.

"And why were you out in the desert, again?" Ben asked.

"We were on a journey. We are looking for a great treasure," I told him.

"Yeah and that's why we're here. We crossed the sea and Ken told us to check in with you or whoever inhabited this lighthouse," Micah added.

"A treasure, eh? Would that be, by any chance, the treasure that's inside the mountain, now is it?" Ben asked.

"That's the one," Micah said.

Ben walked around the room, looking outside the large windows that were on every side of the room. He took a long look through the window that peeked to the mainland.

"It's not worth it, mates. It's a dangerous path up to it. The treasure's been there for quite a while - years maybe. I heard that some crazy admin or mod created the whole thing using a lot of nasty things. The mountain is really tall and big. It's the tallest that any mountain can be in Minecraft and it's guarded by some dangerous things," Ben said.

"What are you talking about?" I asked him.

"Well, Ken didn't tell you much, did he?" Ben asked.

"He told us everything he knew," Jerry told him.

"He did, aye. But I know more. These woods here are filled with creatures like you've never seen before –white monsters," Ben said gloomily.

"What? White monsters? What are you talking about?" Micah asked.

"Well, you all know about zombies and endermen and such, don't you? They come out at night or in the darkness beneath the earth and kill unsuspecting Minecraft players, right? These frozen woods right here are filled with the same monsters, only they're all white and are twice as strong and persistent as the normal ones. Spiders flock in huge numbers, coming out of chasms in the ground. Zombies lurk in packs of twenty or more. Endermen come out of nowhere and can kill you in seconds, some of them even without being provoked. White creepers are even faster and stealthier than normal green ones. Pretty scary, huh?" Ben asked.

"Where do these monsters come from?" I asked Ben.

"Who knows? Who cares? They've been here ever since I built my lighthouse here. There were more of us in the beginning. We had a small town of players. They got driven out of here," Ben said.

"By who?" I asked.

"Well, hostile mobs are dangerous, you see. But hostile players are far more dangerous than any mob," Ben said. "At first, the white monsters didn't bother us that much, they mostly stayed inside the woods, rarely venturing out here on the coast. Normal hostile mobs spawn out here. But then came the players. A clan of players came through here, in search of the dragon's treasure. They came through here and went into the forest, trying to reach the mountain. Things were pretty normal in the days after they left. But it wasn't like that for too long, though. Monsters started coming out of the forest, attacking us when we were out harvesting, invading our mines and killing players left and right. The monsters were always led by at least one player – a player from that clan that went through here. After some time, the attacks stopped. There were only four of us left, that's why you saw those houses outside. After a while, Minecraft wasn't that fun anymore, so my friends left this world. I'm the only one here. It's quiet and I can build my experiments in peace," Ben said.

"Whoa…why did the players from the clan do that? How…I mean…I don't understand…" I said.

"Well, I think that they found what they were looking for up there, up that mountain and they're protecting it. That's why they attacked us – they thought that we were planning to steal their treasure. Once they saw us minding our own business, they let us go. They have no problem with me; they know that I'm not interested in their stupid treasure."

"So how are they in control of the monsters, then?" Micah asked.

"I have no idea, lads," Ben answered.

While we were having this conversation, our new companion, Tom, was standing in the corner silently, probably trying to figure out if he was to keep traveling with us or not.

"Look, I admire your courage in going after this treasure. And I do believe that you lads are friends with Ken. So, I'm going to give you as much as I can in order to help you. I have a stash of things that I keep, in case, you know, I need to make a quick exit. Ken will probably repay me for helping you lot, so no worries. Maybe you can even bring me some treasure, eh? If you lot survive, that is," Ben said, laughing.

He then pulled a lever that opened the way to a secret room. He went inside and after a minute or so he came back out.

"Oi! Here you go! Some food, a diamond pickaxe, some arrows, a lot of torches, some extra iron ingots in case you want to craft yourselves some weapons or tools, and some potions that I've been brewing. You're free to take them all," Ben told us.

"Uh…we're very grateful for your help, Ben, but we don't have any more free space in our inventories," Jerry told him.

"Well, that's not good, is it? You know what? I'm going to give you Berta," Ben said.

"What? Who's Berta?" I asked.

"My donkey, of course. Poor old Berta, she's got containers on her back with plenty of space. Make sure that you treat her well, all right? And I want her back in top shape when you guys are done with your little adventure!" Ben told us.

"Thanks a million, Ben!" I told him.

"Yeah, well, I'm only helping you lot because Ken's such a good friend. Otherwise I would have let my dogs bite you on your behinds while I riddled you with arrows," Ben said, half-jokingly.

Then at that moment, the dogs started violently barking from down below.

Ben looked at us.

"Is this a trap, eh? Are these guys with you?"

"What guys?" Micah asked.

All of us ran up to the window and looked down at the houses below. A rather large group of players clad in iron armors surrounded the camp.

Micah immediately recognized the player that was at the head of the group.

"Zeke! Zeke and his clan are here! What are we going to do?" Micah asked.

We could hear yelling from down below.

"Where is everybody? Anybody home? Come out or we'll burn your houses to the ground!" Zeke yelled.

All of us huddled up and looked back and forth at each other.

"Should we go down there and fight them?" I asked.

"Are you crazy? Don't let this diamond gear fool you, Mike! We're severely outnumbered," Micah said.

"Well we can't sit right here and do nothing! They'll tear down every building one by one until they find someone," Jerry said.

Finally Ben spoke.

"You lads sit tight. I'll go down there and talk to them."

Printed in Great Britain
by Amazon